DREAMWORKS PICTURES AND NICKELODEON MOVIES
P R E S E N T

HOTEL FOR DOGS ™

DESIGNED
FOR
DOGS
AN INVENTOR'S HANDBOOK

by Irene Kilpatrick
based on the book by Lois Duncan
screenplay by Jeff Lowell and Bob Schooley & Mark McCorkle

Simon Spotlight
New York   London   Toronto   Sydney

SIMON SPOTLIGHT
An imprint of Simon & Schuster Children's Publishing Division
1230 Avenue of the Americas, New York, New York 10020
TM Paramount Pictures. © 2008 DreamWorks LLC.
All Rights Reserved. All rights reserved, including the right
of reproduction in whole or in part in any form.
SIMON SPOTLIGHT and colophon are registered
trademarks of Simon & Schuster, Inc.
Manufactured in the United States of America
10 9 8 7 6 5 4
ISBN-13: 978-1-4169-7185-6
ISBN-10: 1-4169-7185-8

Hi! I'm Bruce, and I'm eleven. I guess I'm pretty normal. And I guess I'm also something of an inventor. I love to tinker with things, which helps keep my mind off the fact that I've been in and out of foster homes for the last three years.

Thank goodness for my sister, Andi—she's sixteen—and our dog, Friday. He's a Jack Russell terrier. Foster kids aren't supposed to have pets, so we kept him hidden from our foster families, and our caseworker, Bernie. Bernie is great. He cares about us, and he was really trying to help us to find a forever family.

When we moved in with our latest foster parents, the Scudders, Andi and I decided we would try to make Bernie happy by staying there as long as possible.

We would sneak Friday into our room at night, but he wandered around the Scudders's apartment building during the day. So I invented a device to call him, and that's when he'd come running to get his meals. Friday never missed a meal!

electric can opener is activated and sound is amplified through the megaphone

THE FRIDAY CALLER
- BACK END OF A BICYCLE
- CRANK TURNED BIKE PEDAL
- PEDAL TURNED GEARS
- GEARS TURNED CAN OPENER
- SOUND WAS CARRIED THROUGH AMPLIFIER ON ROOF

One evening, Andi, Friday, and I were just walking around, trying to mind our own business, when some cops thought we were troublemakers. They started to chase us! We all ran—Andi and I following Friday as he dodged through side streets and alleys. He led us straight to a run-down old building—the Hotel Francis Duke.

The hotel seemed empty at first, but we found out right away that it wasn't. Two dogs lived there: Lenny, who was big and slobbery, and his tiny best friend, Georgia.

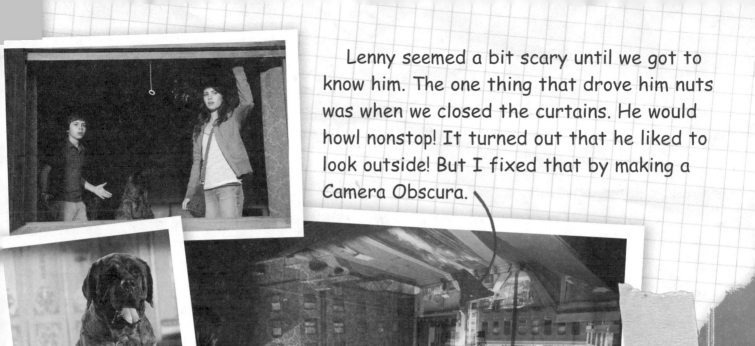

Lenny seemed a bit scary until we got to know him. The one thing that drove him nuts was when we closed the curtains. He would howl nonstop! It turned out that he liked to look outside! But I fixed that by making a Camera Obscura.

I poked a tiny hole in the curtain, then put a glass in front of it. The view from the window came through the hole and showed up upside-down on the opposite wall. Luckily, Lenny didn't mind lying on his back. People have known how to do this for ages, but I think I may have been the first person to use it to make a dog happy!

MY WORKSHOP

Andi and I found an amazing room in the hotel. Well, it was amazing to me, anyway. It was filled with everything I needed to create things, like a fetching machine for Georgia. That girl loves to fetch!

I put together the device out of things I found. With a simple flick, it could launch anything across the room. That kept Georgia busy for hours.

I wished Dad could have seen my workshop and my new inventions. He was the one who taught me how to put things together, and he made me believe that I could do anything I wanted.

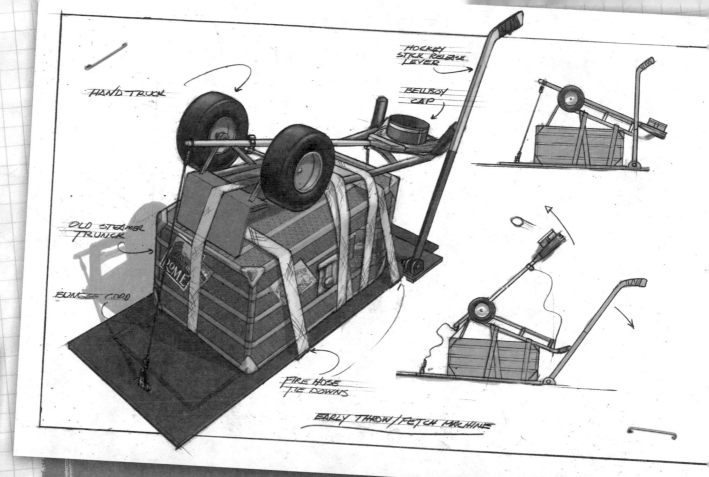

HOCKEY STICK RELEASE LEVER

BELLBOY CAP

HAND TRUCK

OLD STEAMER TRUNK

BUNGEE CORD

ROME

FIRE HOSE TIE DOWNS

EARLY THROW/FETCH MACHINE

THE FLING-AND-FETCH

- STEAMER TRUNK TIED TO OLD DOOR
- HAND TRUCK TIED TO TOP OF TRUNK WITH FIRE HOSE
- BROOM, HANDLE END ATTACHED TO DOOR WITH BUNGEE CORD
- BELLBOY CAP ON BROOM END (TO HOLD OBJECTS)
- HOCKEY STICK LEVER

RELEASE THE LEVER, AND THE BROOM SPRANG FORWARD, THROWING THE OBJECT ACROSS THE ROOM! WORKED LIKE A CATAPULT!

TAKING CARE OF BUSINESS

Andi made some friends at the pet store, and they brought three more dogs. With six dogs living in the hotel, we realized that it might start to smell pretty bad if we didn't figure out what to do with all the doggy poop and pee. Plus we never knew when we would have to stay home with the Scudders. Cleaning the hotel would be a nightmare the next time we came back!

The Pee Room

My first idea was to put a fire hydrant in an old shower stall. When a dog finished peeing, he stepped on a platform that turned on the showerhead. The water washed the hydrant for a few seconds and then turned off. Then it would be clean and ready for the next dog!

Convey-o-Poop

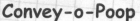

I was pretty proud of this one, if I say so myself! I found a ramp that I placed next to a long table. Then I cut eight holes in the table and put toilet seats over the holes. Under the table I set up a motorized conveyor belt lined with newspaper. After the dogs "did their thing," the poop traveled on the belt to a sheet of shrink-wrap, which wrapped up the package, and then under a hair dryer, which sealed the deal. Then the packages fell out a hole in the wall, right into the Dumpster outside the hotel. No stinky mess!

KEEPING DOGS HAPPY

Each dog liked to do different things, so I built machines to keep them all happy. Cooper, the bulldog, could shred anything to bits. So I turned an old vending machine into a chew toy machine. It went through many changes, but in the end it worked perfectly.

The Masticator

The vending machine was full of Cooper's favorite things, such as shoes and small pillows. Just press the button, and out popped the perfect chew toy!

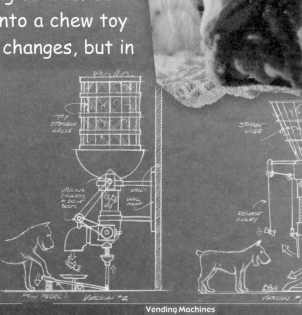

Vending Machines

Shep, a Border collie, constantly needed to keep things organized—dogs and people included. To get her to stop herding us around, I made some mechanical sheep.

Herding Heaven

I found five remote-controlled trucks and cars, and even a bumper car. Attached to each of these was a sheep, which I made out of metal hoops, chicken wire, wood, foam, cloth, and other scraps. My friends and I even added a fake split-rail fence and hand-painted scenery to create a sheep pasture.

Dog Spa

I found a huge industrial dishwasher in the hotel kitchen and turned it into a dog-washing machine. The dog would walk up the ramp and sit on a moving platform. The first stop was the washing, where the dog got soaped up, then rinsed. Then the dog was taken to a drying station, where he sat in the middle of three hair dryers. Once he was dry, he walked down the ramp at the other end.

Romeo was a big fan of our washing and grooming machine—and his new girlfriend, Juliet, loved it just as much as he did!

HOME, SWEET HOME

I wanted to give the dogs the feeling that they were living in a real home with a human family. So I came up with these gadgets!

Newspaper Delivery

One of the things dogs like to do at home is fetch the newspaper. So I rigged up a slidelike thing, with one end placed at the mail slot of a door. On top of the slide was a box filled with newspapers. I filled this box by climbing a ladder I attached to the slide. Lastly, I attached a timer that would trigger the bottom of the box to open and a newspaper to slide out; it made its way down and through the mail slot. Paper's here!

1) DOG SITS ON PEDAL
2) DOOR KNOCKER KNOCKS ON DOOR
3) NEWSPAPER RELEASED DOWN SLIDE AND OUT THROUGH DOOR

ROLLED NEWSPAPER

DOOR KNOCKER

PEDAL

Newspaper/Mail Dispenser

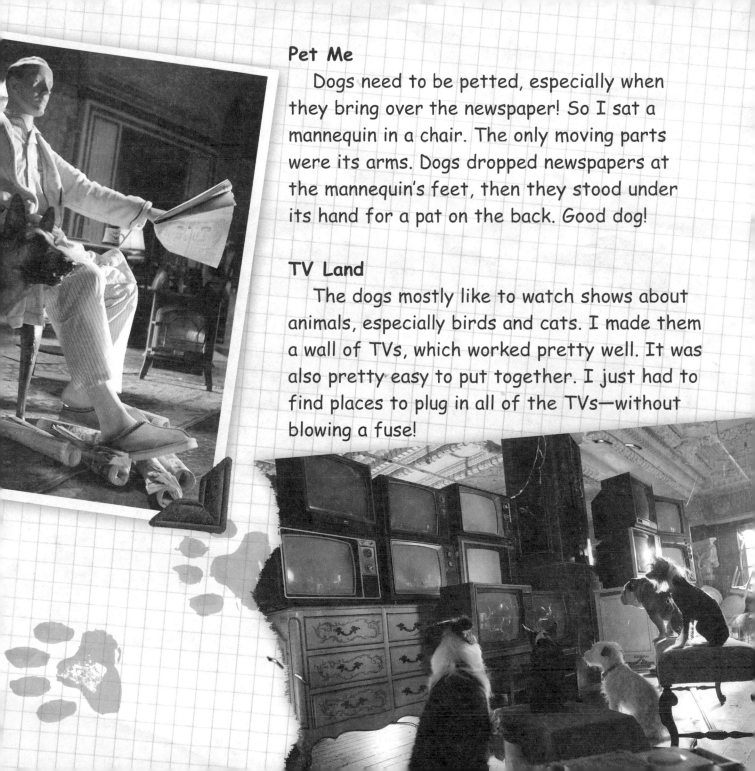

Pet Me

Dogs need to be petted, especially when they bring over the newspaper! So I sat a mannequin in a chair. The only moving parts were its arms. Dogs dropped newspapers at the mannequin's feet, then they stood under its hand for a pat on the back. Good dog!

TV Land

The dogs mostly like to watch shows about animals, especially birds and cats. I made them a wall of TVs, which worked pretty well. It was also pretty easy to put together. I just had to find places to plug in all of the TVs—without blowing a fuse!

A WHOLE LOT OF NOISE

   With so many dogs in one place, it definitely got noisy! To make sure the neighbors didn't hear any barking, howling, or banging, we strapped mattresses to the walls of two rooms to keep them quiet. Here are a couple of machines that were in those rooms. They kept the fun factor and the noise level UP!

KNOCK-KNOCK

- FOUR DOORS ARRANGED IN A CIRCLE
- DOG STEPPED ON MAT IN FRONT OF DOOR
- KNOCKER HIT NEXT DOOR
- DOG RAN TO NEXT DOOR, STEPPED ON MAT
- AND SO ON!

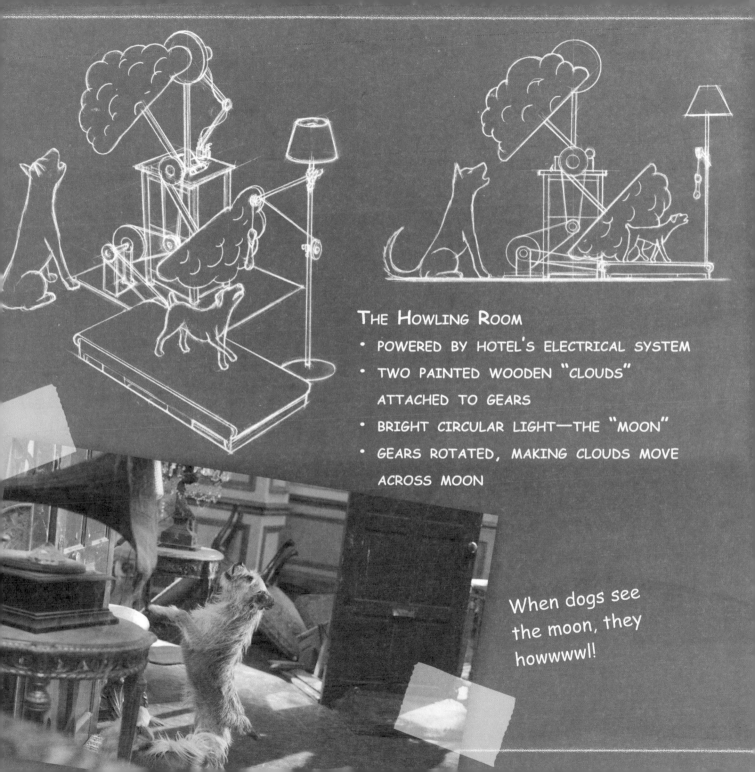

THE HOWLING ROOM

- POWERED BY HOTEL'S ELECTRICAL SYSTEM
- TWO PAINTED WOODEN "CLOUDS" ATTACHED TO GEARS
- BRIGHT CIRCULAR LIGHT—THE "MOON"
- GEARS ROTATED, MAKING CLOUDS MOVE ACROSS MOON

When dogs see the moon, they howwwwl!

ONE DAY . . .

Andi and I always hoped that one day we would find a forever family, one where we would fit right in. We wished the same things for the dogs in the hotel. So I rigged up a couple of things to help them practice for when they found permanent homes.

Pound Pull

This was pretty basic—it was just a spring-loaded mannequin dressed up like a guy from the pound. The dogs ran up and pulled on the rope in the guy's hand. This way, the dogs would be able to escape from the dog catchers next time, and make it home safely.

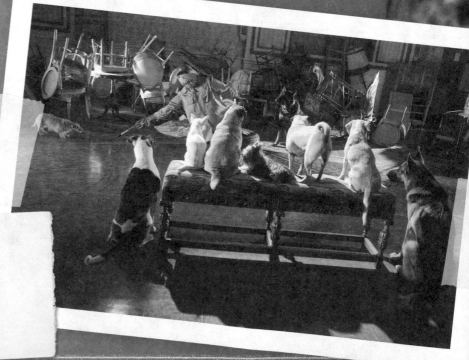

THE WIND-O

- CAR DOOR PROPPED AGAINST CHAIR
- FAN BLEW AIR PAST WINDOW
- DOG SAT ON CHAIR WITH HEAD OUT WINDOW

Just like the real thing!

CHOW TIME!

Every day I worked on the most important task: feeding all the dogs at the hotel! My first version of a feeding machine was for just six dogs. Then as more dogs came to the hotel, I had to make it larger. I didn't want the dogs to ever go hungry or fight over their food!

FEEDING MACHINE

FOR SIX DOGS

- THREE FIVE-GALLON JUGS FULL OF DOG FOOD
- JUGS EMPTIED INTO TUBES THAT CONNECTED TO DOG BOWLS
- DOG PULLED TOY ABOVE BOWL TO GET FOOD

Friday had a lot of fun pulling his toy to get food!

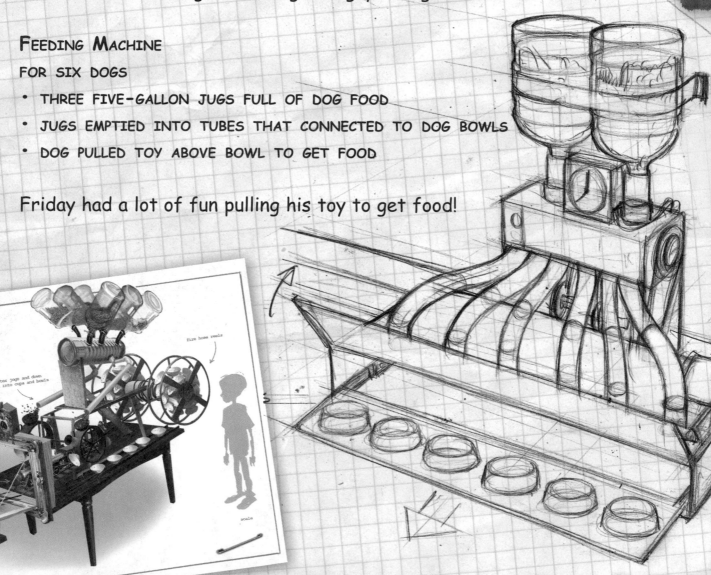

FOR FIFTY DOGS
- CUCKOO CLOCK CONTROLLED MEALTIMES
- TRAIN PULLED DOG BOWLS ALONG TABLE
- DOG-FOOD CANS ROTATED AND DUMPED FOOD INTO BOWLS
- TRAIN HIT BELL AT END OF TABLE—DINNERTIME!

My masterpiece!

BUSTED!

Eventually we got found out. All the dogs—including Friday!—were taken to the pound. Andi and I got split up, but that didn't stop us from trying to find a way to save the dogs.

In the end, it was Bernie who came to everyone's rescue. He convinced the cops and the town to let us turn the hotel into a *real* home for dogs waiting to be adopted.

HOTEL FOR DOGS

F D

Welcome

The best part was when Bernie and his wife, Carol, told us that they were going to be our parents! We were so happy to finally have a home with parents who would really look out for us. We get to spend lots of time at the hotel, finding homes for the dogs. And I still get to make cool new gadgets for the hotel!

STROLL-A-COASTER

ONE OF MY NEWEST INVENTIONS AFTER WE REDECORATED WAS COMING UP WITH THIS GREAT WAY TO GET UP THE STAIRS. THE SMALL DOGS REALLY LOVED THIS! I USED THE OVERHEAD CONVEYOR FROM THE DRY-CLEANING SECTION OF THE LAUNDRY ROOM, RIGGED IT UP TO LOOP UP THE STAIRS OF THE LOBBY, AND PUT FANCY HANDBAGS ON THE HOOKS. IT WAS A FUN AND CLASSY RIDE—PERFECT FOR OUR LUXURIOUS NEW HOTEL FOR DOGS!